ACROSS THE LINE

MICHAEL KINGSWOOD

 Created with Vellum

Contents

About This Book

Bentonville Police Department's top hostage negotiator has seen it all, but even still nothing could prepare him for what he finds when he rolls into a seemingly routine convenience store holdup.

Across the Line is a 4,300 word short mystery.

Enjoy the book! After you're done, please come to Michael's website and sign up for his mailing list at michaelkingswood.com/newsletter-signup/. Guaranteed to be spam free, he uses it to announce new releases and special promotions for his fans.

Across The Line

<hr>

nother nutcase.

It never failed. Every time it looked like Sergeant Cole's Friday was going to be quiet, some joker decided to rob a bank, take hostages in an office building, or do something stupid like that. The perp was almost never seriously interested in hurting anyone, of course. Most times, the hostages were a result of his half-assed plan falling apart, and Cole was able to talk him down without too much trouble.

So when he got the call of shots fired and hostages taken at a Convenience Store at the corner of State Street and Cunningham Boulevard, Cole just rolled his eyes in annoyance.

Really, a Convenience Store? The jackass couldn't at least hit a place that would make it worth all the trouble and effort?

Perps tended to be stupid, otherwise they'd be working as Engineers or something. But still, this sort of caper always made Cole wonder how the perp managed to take a bath without drowning.

Cole took his time, refilling his coffee thermos and hitting the bathroom before donning his blue Bentonville PD jacket over his white polo shirt and khakis. Then he strapped on his sidearm and left the precinct station.

All things considered, it was a beautiful summer day. A few puffy clouds moved slowly across the sky, pushed by a gentle breeze. Though it was already quite warm, the humidity was lower than it had been.

A good day for fishing, but there was no way Cole would be able to cut out early now.

The drive from the precinct to the scene would have been quick even without his siren and lights; it was only about two miles away. All the same, by the time he pulled up, the store was ringed with police cruisers. There were probably twenty cops crouching behind the cars, guns drawn. Looking to the right, Cole wasn't surprised to see a sniper team setting up atop the strip mall across the street.

They probably wouldn't be needed, of course. It almost never came to that.

Putting his cruiser into park, Cole opened the door and got out. He had to maneuver a little bit to get his belly around the steering wheel, a reminder that he really needed to start exercising again, and go back on Weight Watchers.

Muttering to himself, Cole shut the door and walked over to the command station. There, he got a surprise.

The scene commander was Bill Kennedy, dressed as always in a well-pressed Navy-blue business suit with an unobtrusive tie. Bill always looked more like a banker than a cop, but he was shrewd and tough. Cole had come up through the Academy with Bill, and was Godfather to one of his kids. They didn't get to interact very much professionally these days, though, since Bill got promoted and sent to a job in Narcotics.

Why was he here, for a robbery case?

"Hi Bill," said Cole as he walked up.

"Good to see you, Greg," Bill replied, shaking his hand quickly with a firm grip

At Bill's side was Helen Duval, head of the Robbery/Homicide unit. She always looked good, and today was no different. She was sporting a tight-fitting pair of bluejeans and a Bentonville PD polo shirt, very similar to Cole's own, and had her brown hair done up in a bun on the back of her head. Once upon a time, Greg had a thing for her, but that was before he got married and was ruined for women forever. She was busy talking with two uniformed officers, but nodded in greeting to Cole in between issuing orders.

"What brings Narcotics out here, Bill?"

"I've got an undercover in there with the perps. They were supposed to be on their way to a deal, but one of the perps freaked out or something, and it all went to hell."

Cole winced. That was a tough spot. He'd never even considered putting his name in for undercover work, but he respected the hell out of the guys who did. Cole couldn't imagine how those guys did it, day in day out, without losing themselves in the criminal world. Truth be told, some did cross the line, but it was a very small minority, much fewer than Cole would have thought.

"I guess we'll have to be extra careful on this one then," he said. "Let's have a look."

He and Bill left the command post and moved up to the ring of cruisers. As they crouched down behind one of the car hoods for cover, Bill handed him a pair of binoculars. Peering through, he could barely make out details inside the store through the tinted windows. Shelves of items for sale, a few signs...nothing really stood out. Wait.

He saw some movement, a shadowy figure walking down one of the aisles.

"Ok, I think I see one of the perps. Any idea where the hostages are?"

Bill shook his head, but before he could speak Helen joined them, interjecting.

"We haven't made contact yet, Sergeant, but we'll have the phone hooked up in a minute. We'll use the normal protocol, I assume?"

"I don't see why not…"

Cole froze. As he was lowering the binoculars, he noticed one of the cars parked in front of the store: a red Ford Focus. Oh no… Raising the binoculars back up to his eyes, he read the license plate, and his heart sank. "Oh my God."

He could feel Helen and Bill's eyes boring into him, though he didn't take his eyes away from the eyepieces.

"What, Greg? What's wrong?"

Cole could hear the tension in Bill's voice, matching the sudden fright he felt himself. He realized he was shaking, and lowered the binoculars. "That's my son's car," Cole said, and was surprised to hear his voice quavering.

Bill breathed a curse. "Can you do this, Greg? We can get someone else."

Cole snorted. "Who, Webster? He couldn't find his ass with two hands. No, I can handle it. I hope."

Looking back at them, Cole could see the doubt in both Bill and Helen's eyes. Particularly Helen's. The two of them exchanged a look, then Helen said, "How about we call him in anyway, just in case."

Righteous indignation flooded Cole in a rush. Where did they get off second-guessing him? He was the best negotiator on the force, and…and he was forced to admit that they were right to be concerned. His thoughts kept going back to Jeffrey, all of seventeen years old, no doubt terrified by what was going on inside the store. Reluctantly, Cole nodded.

"Ok, call him in. But he's here in an assisting role only, agreed?"

Both of them nodded.

"Now where's that phone?"

The three of them straightened and walked back to the command van. As they arrived, technicians were just finishing hooking up the portable telephone equipment. One of the technicians nodded to Cole and handed him the receiver. "Should be coming online now," the tech said. Sure enough, a dial tone issued from earpiece. It only took a moment to get the number to the phone inside the store, then Cole dialed it in and waited.

No one picked up after five rings, but Cole didn't hang up. As he listened to the ring tones continuing, he imagined what was going on inside. The perps debating amongst themselves whether to answer or not. The hostages, his son, cowering in the back corner fearing what the perps would do next. The perps, becoming annoyed with the ringing, beginning to argue more heatedly until they finally dared one of their group to pick up the phone…

Right on cue, someone answered.

"Who is this?" asked a gruff, but young, male voice.

"This is Sergeant Gregory Cole of the Bentonville Police Department. Who am I speaking to?"

"Carl."

"Ok Carl, how is everyone in there?"

"How do you think, Sergeant Cole? We…"

In the background, Cole heard another voice speaking. "Oh shit, that's my…"

"Jeff, shut the fuck up," said Carl, though his voice was muffled as though he was halfway covering the mouthpiece with his hand. But that was all Cole needed to hear. He'd know that voice anywhere. Cole's blood went like ice water, and he almost dropped the phone. Somehow, he didn't know how, he maintained his composure and managed a professional tone.

"Carl, put Jeff on the line."

There was a long pause. Cole could hear the wheels turning in the perp's head. In his mind's eye, Cole could picture Carl, whoever he was, and Jeffrey trading looks. Jeffrey shaking his head, wanting nothing more than to avoid talking with his father through that phone line. Carl licking his lips as hope that maybe an inside connection could get them out of this bloomed in his mind.

Finally, Cole heard Carl say softly, "He wants to talk to you." Then a moment later, his son's voice spoke to him over the phone.

"Dad?"

"Yeah Jeff, it's me. What the hell's going on? What are you doing mixed up in this?"

He could feel Bill and Helen's gazes again. Glancing to the side, Cole saw their expressions: Bill looking stricken, Helen looking resigned but determined. They could both hear the conversation over the speakers attached to the phone line.

Jeffrey's voice was strained. It sounded like he was barely holding back tears. "Sorry, dad. Scott and me just wanted some pot for the party tomorrow. But things got nuts, and…"

There was a moment of scuffling around on the other end of the line, then the sound of muffled voices conversing. No doubt Carl and the others didn't like that Jeffrey had revealed that much, and were trying to silence him. Finally, Jeffrey came back on the line.

"Listen, Dad..."

"No, you listen, son. I've told you how these things work. You guys are in a no-win situation here. You need to just come out and give up before someone gets hurt."

"Can't do that."

"Jeffrey..."

"No. Tell the cops to pull back. We'll get in my car and drive away. No one gets hurt, and we all go our separate ways."

The phone went dead.

"Son of a bitch," Cole breathed. For once, he knew he was telling the truth when he said that, considering his ex-wife was Jeffrey's mother.

Bill clapped him on the shoulder. "Greg, Webster will be here in a minute. You need to get off this case right now." Beside him, Helen was nodding in agreement.

Cole shook his head.

"I mean it, Greg. You can't do a negotiation with your own son and you know it."

Cole ground his teeth, the fear for Jeff's safety combined with anger at Bill's words causing the telltale ache in his belly that presaged a flareup of acid reflux. Problem was, Bill was right. Deny it all he wanted, there was no way Cole could go about this case dispassionately. If he stayed on there was a good chance folks, maybe Jeff, would get hurt or worse.

Slowly, reluctantly, Cole nodded and set the phone down. He took a step back and found himself on the ground before he even realized his legs had given out on him.

Bill and Helen were down with him in a heartbeat, concern written deeply on their faces. "You ok, Greg?" Bill asked.

Cole nodded, holding back a wince as his reflux began kicking in big-time. "Tell Webster to hurry his ass up."

IT TOOK Webster an eternity to get to the scene.

Or at least it felt like an eternity to Cole. He managed to get back to his feet long enough to maneuver into one of the folding chairs that were set up in the command post. Then he downed some Pepto from the bottle he kept in his briefcase and settled down to wait.

The uniformed cops were fully settled into position, their ring around the store complete, by the time Webster arrived, looking disheveled. He had apparently been on the other side of town dealing with a domestic disturbance gone bad. That accounted for his delay in getting here.

Any other day, Cole would have understood completely. But today…

Webster walked up, his ugly green tie clashing with the blue Bentonville PD jacket he habitually wore. That did nothing to make Cole feel any better. If Webster couldn't even tell what kind of tie to wear with what - hell if he hadn't had the good sense to marry a woman who would talk him down from that ledge rather than push him further out onto it - he really did not have the sense to run a scene like this. Not with Cole's son wrapped up in the middle of it.

To his credit though, Webster looked genuinely concerned as he approached. "Jesus, Greg, you must feel like hell," he said. "Don't worry; we'll get Jeff out of there safe and sound."

Cole bit back a sarcastic retort and stood up, shaking Webster's hand. At least the guy had a good grip.

"Thanks, Sam," Cole said, and was surprised to find that he meant it. Webster might not be the sharpest knife in the drawer, but Cole was forced to admit he meant well and always tried, even when he fucked things up. And right then, he was the best option for Jeff's safety.

Webster smiled encouragingly and turned toward where Bill and Helen waited by the phone. The three gathered in a huddle for a few minutes. Their words did not carry to Cole's ears.

He found himself scowling. They were keeping him out of the loop, and it galled. It was also the right call. He was not a cop, not right now. He was a concerned family member of one of the host—Cole caught himself mid-thought and scowled even deeper. He was the concerned family member of one of the perps.

His own son. A fucking perp.

How had Jeff gone so wrong? How had Cole let it happen?

Or had he *made* it happen somehow?

Cole sank back in his chair and looked away from his colleagues. Staring at nothing, he let his thoughts wander back through the months and years past, trying to figure out what he had done that had helped set his son down the wrong path.

He thought of Margaret, Jeff's mother. Cast-iron bitch, almost from the beginning. Or at least once she had her claws dug into Cole good and deep. And then once she had enough years of marriage to get a cut of his pension, she vanished on him. On them. Cole heard she was banging some card player in Vegas these days, but he had no idea if that was true.

He wanted to say he didn't care, but it still stung. In spite of the God-awful way she had treated him for the last ten years or so, somewhere inside she was still the girl Cole had fallen for.

It must have been worse for Jeff. Cole had seen all the signs: Jeff had drawn in on himself, his grades had fallen, he got into fights at school. But after a year or so, he had come back around, and Cole thought he was, if not over it at least adjusted to it, accepting their new situation. In the two years since, things had gotten better and it looked like everything between the two of them, at least, was back to normal and the future bright.

Apparently not.

Maybe if Margaret had not left. If Cole had not driven her off...

He snorted out a bitter half-laugh. If anything, she had tried to drive *him* off, if truth be told. She was only interested in one thing, and once she got it...

"Ah crap," Cole muttered.

Someone was going to have to tell Margaret what was going on with Jeff. That was not going to be a fun phone call.

With a sigh, Cole dug his cell phone out of the inner pocket of his jacket then walked away from the command station for some privacy. He had Margaret's mother's phone number still - kids still like grandma even if Mom is a bitch. She might know how to get in touch with her wayward daughter.

This was not going to be a fun call at all.

Turns out, it was even worse than Cole thought it would be.

WHEN COLE finally returned to the command station, he felt like he'd been whipped up one side and back down the other. Bill noticed immediately and raised an eyebrow at him, questioning.

"I talked to Margaret," Cole said.

"Ah."

There was nothing else to say about it, so Cole did not. Bill didn't press the issue. Bless him.

"What's the status in there?"

Bill frowned and turned his gaze on the store. "Haven't heard from them in a while, but Webster thinks they're starting to lose resolve."

"What do you think?"

Bill cleared his throat and glanced at Webster, who was talking with Helen down by the ring of cruisers in front of the store. His frown got deeper. Cole's heart sank.

His expression must have given him away, because Bill spoke quickly. "Doesn't matter what I think, Greg. You need to remain positive." He took a breath and smiled. It was the carefully practiced, false, smile that Greg had seen, and used himself, dozens of times when the situation was dire and you didn't want to panic a family member. "Everything will be fine, Greg," he said. "Honest."

Cole returned the smile in kind. "Ok. Thanks, buddy."

For a moment, he indulged in the fantasy that either of them believed a word of it. The moment did not last.

A shot rang out.

At first Cole thought one of the uniformed cops had screwed up, discharged his weapon by accident. Or at least he wanted to think that; hoped for it. But that moment passed quickly. The shot had come from the convenience store.

All around, cops pulled their weapons and took

cover behind their cruisers, watching the store with rapt attention.

Nothing happened for several eternal seconds. Then the front door of the convenience store swung open and a figure stumbled out.

It was getting on toward evening; the sun was low on the horizon, casting long shadows from the nearby buildings, and the convenience store faced east. So at first it was hard to make out anything from the person except that it looked male and he was bent over, clutching at his belly with both hands as he stumbled forward several steps toward the ring of police cruisers.

Then he fell to the ground face-first.

He cried out, a long low groan of pain and fear that carried across the intervening space clearly, and Cole could see he was trying to crawl toward the cops, but he did not make fast progress.

Cole got a better look at the man's clothing, jeans and a green short-sleeved collared shirt, sneakers. It reminded him of the sort of thing Jeff wore...

Oh no.

Oh dear Lord no.

Cole looked closer. The sandy-colored hair, hanging loose to shoulder length. That green shirt...wasn't it the one Cole's mother had given him for his birthday?

No, it couldn't be.

Then he heard the moan, louder this time. More clear.

"Dad."

COLE WAS across the parking lot in a flash, heedless of the shouts from his fellow officers, and crouched down next to his son. He was aware of tears running down his cheeks, but it he paid them no mind. His only focus was on Jeff, the boy he'd held as a baby, the kid he'd played baseball with, the young man he was proud to send off to the prom.

And now the victim of a gunshot wound to the gut, bleeding out on the pavement in front of a convenience store.

All because some pissants wanted to go get stoned.

Cole helped his son roll over onto his back. He knew you weren't supposed to move an injured person but… He couldn't just leave him face-down in the street. As the wound came into view, Cole felt his breath catch in his throat. Jeff's belly was ripped open almost someone had taken a sword to it. The shot must have grazed him instead of hitting him straight-on. It must have been a larger caliber bullet, though; Cole thought he could see some of Jeff's guts trying to come out.

Terror, couple with rage, swept through him. Which was the stronger? Did it matter? They fought within Cole's soul, tearing at each other in their quest to devour him. His head whirled and he could not see for a moment.

And then all he felt was cold.

Jeff clutched at his arm with one hand - he needed the other to hold his guts in. His eyes were terrified, pleading, remorseful. "Dad, I'm sorry."

Cole said something. He wasn't sure what, but it seemed to do the trick. Jeff slumped back onto the ground, some of the guilt fading from his eyes. And did he manage a smile? No, that was a trick of the eye. Shot people don't smile.

Then he went still.

Cole heard a guttural roar, the kind of cry a

beast makes. It took a moment for him to realize the roar was coming from his own mouth. He moved more quickly than he ever thought he could have, getting to his feet and rushing the convenience store door.

He had his sidearm in his hands, but had no memory of drawing it.

Somewhere in the background, people were shouting his name, ordering him to stop. It was like so many buzzing flies, just noise.

Then he was through the door.

He swept the store over the sights of his gun. A huddled cluster of people in the back corner. The hostages. A trio of men standing in a circle in front of the cooler section. They were shouting at each other. One of them held a semi-automatic handgun in his hand. Cole thought he could still see smoke rising from the muzzle.

The three men turned as one, shocked surprise on their faces.

The gunman's eyes widened and he began to raise the weapon. Cole didn't realize he had fired until the man's - the boy's really - head kicked back and the cooler behind him became splattered with blood and brain matter.

Cole turned his gun on the second man, a spindly little guy of maybe sixteen. Cole thought he might have recognized him from Jeff's school at some point.

The kid looked terrified. Cole shot him without a second thought.

Only one perp remained. He had his hands up. There was something in his left hand that flashed gold.

"I'm a cop!" he shouted, waving his left hand around frantically.

"You let them kill my son," Cole said.

Then he pulled the trigger.

COLE SAT in the back of a police cruiser, his hands cuffed behind his back. His thoughts were awhirl. The entire incident was surreal, like he had witnessed it through someone else's eyes.

But it was real. He had done it.

The white-hot rage, the coldness, had faded, leaving Cole only with the disbelief over what he had done. The guilt, threatening to crush his soul.

The satisfaction.

The passenger side front door opened and Bill climbed into the car. He sat in the seat, silently, for a long minute or so. Cole could see from his profile that he was working his jaw the way he did when he could not decide whether he was pissed or scared or what.

Cole could relate.

Finally Bill turned around and Cole was surprised to see tears in his friend's eyes. "Jesus, Greg."

Cole shrugged his shoulders, as much as he could with his hands cuffed as they were. What did Bill expect him to say, that he was sorry? He knew he should be, but he wasn't. Not really.

They sat in silence for a while, just looking at each other. The silence spoke volumes.

Then Bill inhaled quickly through his nose and wiped his eyes. "Paramedics finished up with Jeff."

Cole nodded. It hadn't taken them long; but then how much time does it take to give aid to a dead person?

"He's going to be ok, Greg."

Wait. What? Cole felt his jaw drop open. What had Bill said? Against his better judgment, Cole felt hope blossom within him. Was it possible? No. He had seen - had *felt* - Jeff die. "What?"

Bill leaned forward. "He's going to be ok." He spoke the words slowly, with emphasis, as though trying to force them into Cole's head. "They're taking him to surgery, but they think they got to him in time and the Docs'll be able to patch him up. It'll be a tough recovery, but they seemed optimistic he'll be up and about good as new in a few months."

It was like a ten ton weight had been lifted. Cole breathed deeply, as though he had been underwater for five minutes. It felt like the first breath he had drawn in his life.

He was shaking, there in the car seat. Then he realized he was weeping, with relief, with joy.

"I don't know what we're going to do with you, Greg," Bill said. "Whether to give you a medal or bring you up on charges. Maybe both."

The words washed over Cole, but he paid them little heed. Whatever else came from this night, his son was going to be ok. That was all that mattered.

Cole kept on crying. Slowly, though, his tears became laughter, and before long all that was all he could hear.

Bill watched him for a time, his expression that of a man who's not sure whether he is looking at madman or not. Then he opened the car door and got out.

Cole's laughter followed him.

Thank you for reading my book. I hope you enjoyed reading it as much as I enjoyed writing it.

Every review helps an author out, so whether you loved this book, hated it, or something in between, please take a minute to tell other readers what you thought. All of the online retailers make it very easy to do, and I would really appreciate it.

Feel free to come say hi at my website or on Facebook. I always enjoy hearing from readers, especially since you all are, collectively, my boss.

I also have a weekly podcast, Story Time With Michael Kingswood, where I read stories and talk through some of the latest goings on in my world. I'd love to see you there.

Thanks again. My best to you and yours.

Warm Regards,
Michael Kingswood

Mailing List

If you enjoyed this book and would like word on new releases and special deals from Michael Kingswood, sign up for his newsletter on his website. Guaranteed to be spam-free, you can opt out at any time. And you can rest assured he will not share your information with anyone, for any reason.

https://michaelkingswood.com/newsletter-signup/

About The Author

Michael Kingswood is 20-year veteran of the US Navy submarine force and a lifelong fan of science fiction and fantasy literature. His work has appeared in numerous collections and anthologies, to include the Fiction River Anthology series from WMG publishing. He holds a bachelors degree in Mechanical Engineering as well as a Master of Engineering Management and a Master of Business Administration. He has four children and currently resides in San Diego.

Find Michael Kingswood online at:

www.michaelkingswood.com

www.facebook.com/michael.kingswood

steemit.com/@michaelkingswood

The Champion

Veritas Morte

Story Collections

Tales Of Adventure #1

Tales Of Adventure #2

Short Story 10-Pack

A Jar Of Mixed Treats

Short Fiction

Michael has also published a number of shorter works,
links to which can be found on his website.